I0580311

The Yaffingale's Tale

A Magical Tale
Written & Illustrated By

Kathy Sharp

All rights reserved, no part of this publication
may be either reproduced or transmitted
by any means whatsoever without the prior
permission of the publisher

Text and Illustrations © Kathy Sharp
Cover image © Kathy Sharp

Edited by Kelli Hill

ISBN: 978-1-916756-22-9

November 2024

VENEFICIA PUBLICATIONS UK
veneficiapublications.com

This story is for Nina, who had the idea for a 'tree book' as we stood under a beautiful beech tree in Stourhead Gardens between lockdowns in 2020.

The story, and the tales-within-the-tale are inspired by a set of runes I came across online. The runes have various meanings, and I chose the ones that suited me best, so off you go, and follow the story from Chaos to Blessings.

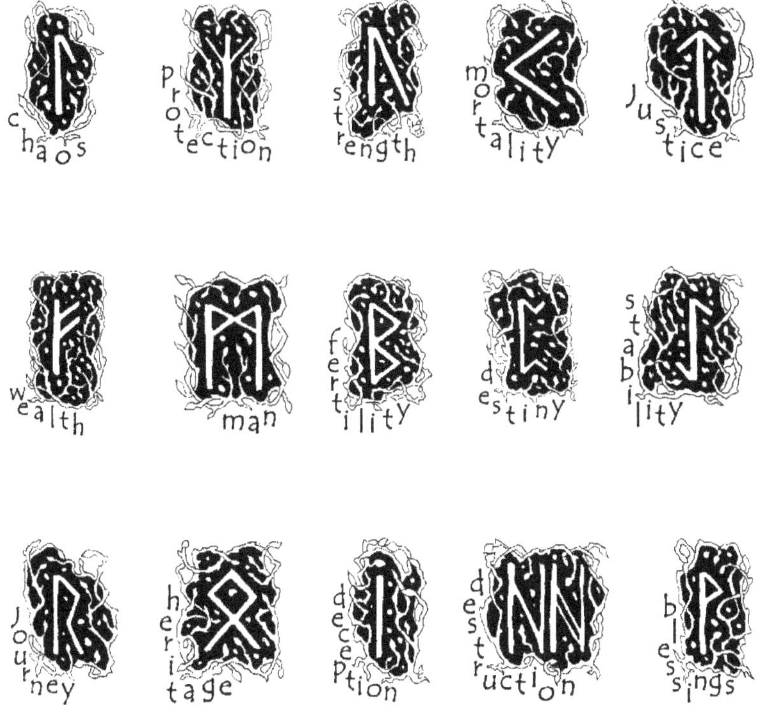

Contents

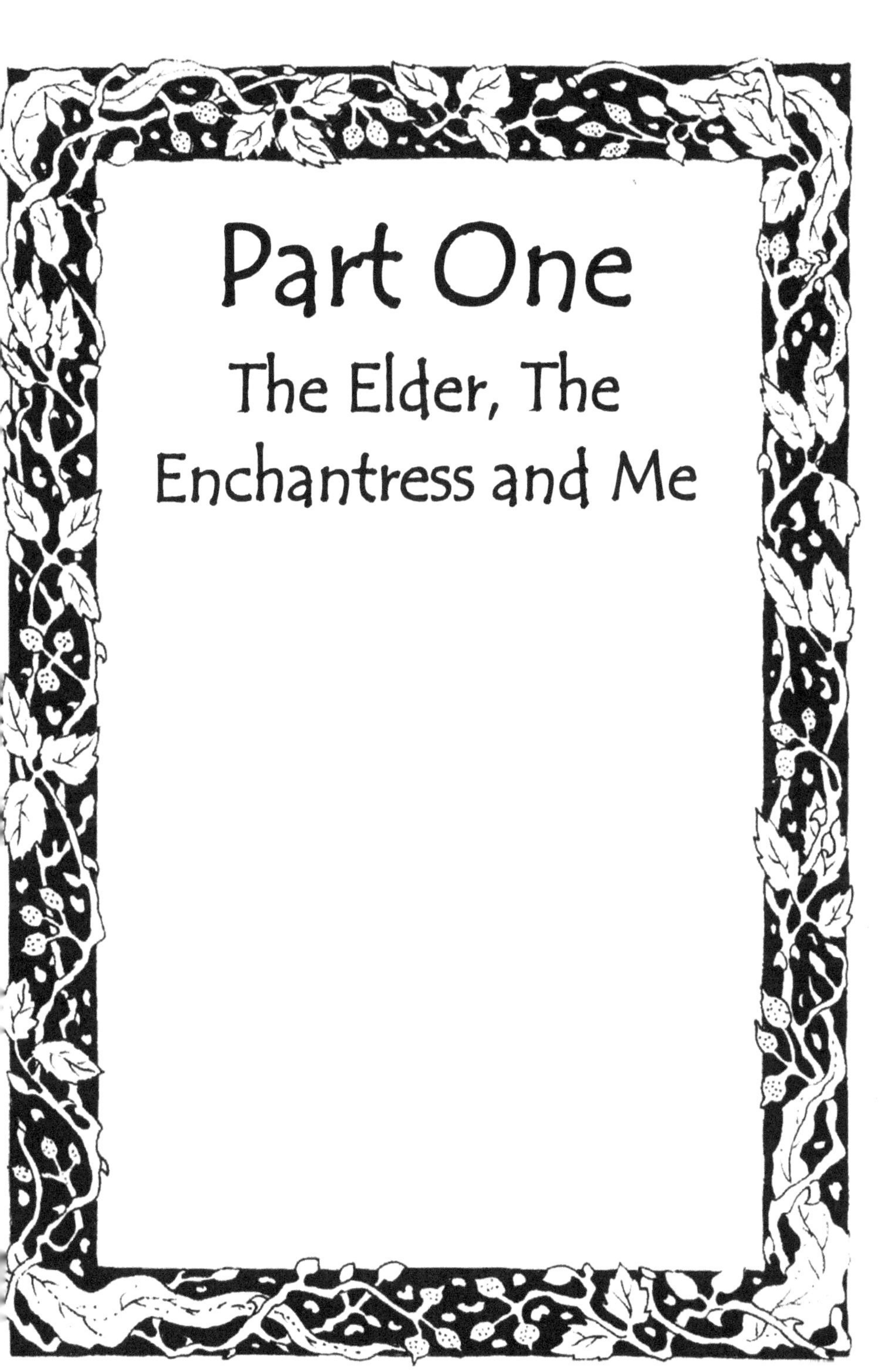

Part One

The Elder, The Enchantress and Me

The Yaffingale

Inspired by the green woodpecker (Picus viridis), a bird with many folk names, including rainbird, yaffle or yaffingale.

To begin with, I am now a very aged woodpecker. Not so young as I used to be, for sure, but like most other aged beings I have a story to tell, and a very odd one at that. Much of it is strange, some of it is dangerous, and most of it is magic. It happened when I was young and green in every way.

*

It began when I landed on a little tree in search of something to eat. A bark beetle would go down well, I thought. The bark was soft and loose. Easy to shift. I began to lever it off. Easy work.

There was a sharp intake of breath.

'Do you mind?' said a voice in my ear, very cross. I nearly fell off the little tree.

'It's bad enough being trapped in this thing without people poking about in your undergarments.'

'Sorry,' I said, taken aback, 'I shouldn't have intruded if I'd known the tree were occupied—much less somebody's undergarments.'

'I should think so, too.' She sounded mollified. 'You've got your foot in my ear, by the way. Sharp claws. Very uncomfortable.'

I hopped a little way along the branch. I had disturbed an elder witch, I realised, and there was no telling what form her retribution might take. Best remain respectful.

'I'll just move on, shall I?' I said. Discretion is the better part of valour, after all.

'Not so fast, Master Yaffingale,' she said. There was a sneakiness in her tone that made me uneasy. 'Since you're here, perhaps you can help me. Problem is very simple, even for a bird-brain such as yourself.' I ignored this blatant insult, and she went on. 'I am locked in, you see. Cannot find the means to get out. Most annoying, you'll agree.'

I thought locked-in was probably the best place for her, but I cocked a sympathetic ear. One wouldn't wish to be turned into a mushroom just for not listening.

'The tree bark,' she said. 'There is a mechanism in the bark that will release me.

And you, sir, as a woodpecker, would be very well placed to find it. Oblige me by having a look, will you? Just mind where you put your beak.'

The elder was a skinny old tree, and I spotted the mechanism, grown into the bark, straight away; it was marked with a symbol.

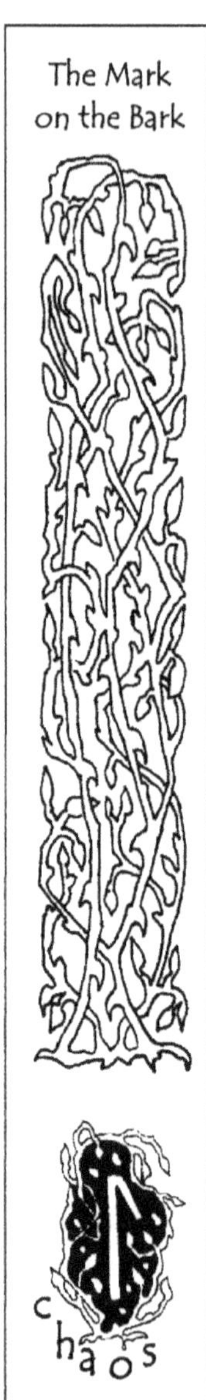

Now, I don't read. I'm a woodpecker, not a man of letters, but I assumed it meant Way Out or Door, or something like that. But was it wise to let her out, even if I could? Someone might have had a very good reason for shutting her in. I hesitated.

'I see you've found it,' she said.

Damn it, she must have had one of her eyes in a knot-hole.

'Um, yes,' I said, 'but I don't know how it works.

'Just have a peck at it, you idiot. Do something.'

I pecked the symbol and launched myself into the air; and in the nick of time, too. The mechanism was released and out she came, whooping, in a sheet of flame.

Had I known that she was not just a common-or-garden elder witch but a dangerous enchantress,

I would never have let her out of the tree in the first place.

No indeed. I've had plenty of time to regret it. But I did let her out. Mea culpa. My own fault.

'I shan't forget you, Master Yaffingale,' she yelled as she went. 'I shall leave you a little gift.'

I had no idea whether that was a thank-you or a dire threat.

It was a while later that I realised that I understood the true meaning of the mark on the bark. Was that the gift, knowledge? If it was, it was one I could do without. That mark meant chaos, and I had unleashed it.

The Elder

Inspired by the elder (Sambucus nigra), a tree with much folklore attached to it, deserved or not. Among its many interesting features, it has ears. Well, not real ones; they are fungi called jelly ears (Auricularia auricula-judae), but that's an interesting thing for a tree to have, don't you think?

I really should have stayed away from that part of the wood after that, but my curiosity got the better of me and I went back to the old elder-tree, and I asked about the witch. It turned out to be a chatty tree and told me the whole story.

'Allow me to introduce myself,' said the tree, 'I am the elder, only a small tree by nature, I am, but such scandalous things they say about me! Bitter fruit, they say. Well, yes. Bitter. But, I say, it makes very good wine, if only you have the patience.

But mostly people don't have the patience. They just carry on complaining. Furthermore, they say my flowers smell of cat's pee. They make excellent wine, too, I say, but my remark about patience applies to that, too.

There is no pleasing some people.

They say, too, that it's bad luck to burn my wood in their houses. That would be bad luck for me, certainly, so I'll go along with that one. I've no intention of ending my days as soot up a chimney.

But there are more scurrilous suggestions. They say a traitor hanged himself from my branches. He must have been a very small traitor, I say, to have done that, given my lack of height. They take no notice of that, obvious though it is, and go on spreading horrid rumours about me.

They say a witch lives inside me. Scandalous. But in this instance, true, though I don't admit it in public. I can indeed accommodate a witch, and I have. You see, Master Yaffingale, she was not merely your workaday witch, but a great enchantress, and a great trial to me, too, I might add. What was she doing in my trunk and branches, you ask? It's a long story, but I will try to be brief.

Once upon a time there was a plague visited on the rye fields in these parts.

When people ate the rye, they had visions of fire and fancied their limbs in flames. Some of them died from the fright.

The enchantress passed by, and the people blamed her – said she had put a curse on the crop out of sheer spite. She denied it, of course.

Now I am not sure, Master Yaffingale, whether she was being truthful or not. It's difficult to tell. The first I heard of it was when they brought her to me, bundled up in her own robes, and tied her to my trunk. I let them do it. Why not? But when they brought kindling and piled it round her and me, and then brought fire brands in, I realised they were going to burn her, and me with her. Well, I wasn't having that. Whether she caused the plague or not is immaterial; it wasn't my fault. So I whisked her into my trunk and branches. Not a very good fit for either of us, but the people saw she had vanished, and they went away. And there she remained until you so kindly let her out. I couldn't do it myself, you see.

But consider this; they had no real reason to burn her. The enchantress was passing by, everyone knows she is powerful and bad-tempered – but that doesn't mean she caused the plague. That is faulty logic. Perhaps a spell slipped out of her grasp. Maybe. But she was guilty then of carelessness, not evil intent. Or maybe the plague was nothing to do with her at all. I've had plenty of time to think about it.

Anyway, it was soon after she arrived, by the by, that the ears appeared. I never had them before.

Of course not. Trees don't have ears. But now I do.

Whether she magicked them onto my dead branches in revenge for entrapping her, I can't tell. I thought I was doing her a favour when I took her in, and see how she repays me.'

The elder-tree fell silent.

'She's not the grateful type,' I said.

'That's true,' said the elder.

'And what's more, she's not trustworthy. You learn quite a lot about a person when she's trapped in your trunk for years on end, you know. I would like to ask a favour of you, Master Yaffingale.'

I was doubtful. Was it wise to do any more favours?

'What is it you want?'

'I am so cut off from the world here,' said the elder, sadly. 'It is the great sadness of a tree's ife that we cannot wander the forest. But you can, good sir. I would wish you to be my ears and eyes. Follow the enchantress. See where she goes and what she does. Visit the other trees and bring back news of her. I suspect she'll be up to no good.'

'It's a dangerous job,' I said. 'She's got a spiteful streak. What's in it for me?'

'I know where all the best anthills are.' The elder had found my weak spot. 'You do like ants, don't you?'

'Love 'em,' I said. 'When do I start?'

And that is how my new career as a spy began.

The Enchantress

Inspired by the enchanter's nightshade (Circaea lutetiana), a plant of shady places and the woodland edge. It is said to be named after the enchantress Circe.

I stuck an eye round the corner of the trunk, and there coming towards me, gliding—I'm not sure her feet were on the ground—was the witch. It had taken me a while to find her, but now I was unsure what to do next. I zipped back to the far side of the trunk. I didn't want to get in her way, but I could just peer round and see what she was up to. Little trails of white mushrooms followed her, sprouting through the ground. I'm not sure she was aware of this, and I was certainly not going to be the one to tell her. I imagined she could be pretty nasty when she was cross.

As she got close, I could see her robes were ragged, probably from all that time shut in the elder tree. That was doing nothing for her temper, either.

I took another glance round the trunk and she caught my eye. It was an unpleasant moment. She was pale and furious, especially seen close up.

I made myself scarce, as you can imagine, but not before I glimpsed her hopping into the hollow trunk of an oak. You'd think she'd had enough of tree trunks, but in she went, quite voluntary, feet first.

After a moment her head popped back up and she called, 'Hey you, Yaffingale. I know you're there. Stop lurking and come here at once. I want a word.'

I looked round the trunk again, just so she could see me.

'Can I help you?' I said.

'I don't trust that elder-tree,' she said, very grumpy. 'It's put me under some sort of enchantment. Very sneaky. But I don't know what it is. I want you to find out.'

Well, I wasn't expecting that. I was so surprised I blurted out the truth.

'As a matter of fact, the elder-tree feels much the same about you, madame. It has sent me to spy on you.'

It was an all-or-nothing moment.

'Has it now?' she said, glaring at me. 'I suppose you had better decide which of us you are working for, Master Yaffingale.'

What could I say?

'You are a great enchantress, madame. I will do whatever you say.'

Right answer,' she said.

'Do whatever the elder asks you, but keep me informed. Understand?'

I understood. Life had suddenly become very complicated. I was now a double agent.

I flew off out of her reach and spotted an anthill in a little glade. Time for lunch, I thought, and began to feast on the ants. I knew I must return to the elder-tree soon and make my report. But what could I say? That tree has magical properties – even the enchantress thought it had put a spell on her. What might it do to a simple woodpecker that attempted to be deceitful?

'Honesty is the best policy,' said a little voice.

I nearly choked on an ant.

'Who's there?' I called. I looked all around the glade, but I couldn't see anything that might have spoken. Was the world going mad, or was it just me? I went back to the ants. Perhaps I had just imagined it. Either way, honesty was probably not the best policy. I would have to be very careful indeed.

When I returned to the elder, it was impatient for news.

'Well,' said the tree, 'did you find the enchantress or not?'

I decided to tell the truth as far as possible.

'Yes,' I said. 'She has settled in the trunk of the lightning-struck oak. At the top of the hill.' All true.

'Did you speak with her?'

'I did. She thinks you have put her under an enchantment.' That was true, too.

'Anything else?'

'No.' Not true. I decided to take a chance. 'Did you really put her under an enchantment?'

The elder was quiet for so long, I thought it had gone to sleep. At last it said, 'Not saying I did. Not saying I didn't.'

'None of my business, I'm sure,' I said. But at least I had something to tell the enchantress now, however unsatisfactory.

'Hmm,' said the elder. 'Right. Now then, Yaffingale, I want you to take yourself off and talk to the trees.'

'Pardon?' I said.

'They can all talk, if they choose. Go and find an oak to begin with – a sensible one, not the lightning-blasted one. That one's probably not in its right mind after an accident like that. Find a sound, sensible oak and ask what the enchantress is up to. Then report back to me.'

I bowed politely. I wasn't sure if the elder could actually see me, but politeness is always a good idea when dealing with magical beings. And away I went, wondering how long it would be before one of them – elder or enchantress would turn me into an earthworm. Or an ant.

Part Two

The Marks on the Bark
and
the Trials in the Tales

The Oak

Inspired by the English oak (Quercus robur), a tree particularly prone to lightning strikes, probably because it's usually the tallest. It's also prone to fungi on its trunk, notably the alarming-looking beefsteak fungus (Fistulina hepatica) which strongly resembles raw meat or a piece of liver, and drips red juice to add to the illusion. It is also often accompanied by the oak milkcap (Lactarius quietus).

I left it a few days, and then set off in the general direction of the lightning-struck oak, but kept my distance. I didn't want to bump into the enchantress before I'd decided just what it was safe to tell her.

I chose a big, strong, sound oak-tree and perched on one of its boughs.

'Good morning,' I said, unsure if there would be a reply.

'Same to you,' said the oak in a booming voice.

'Oh,' I said, 'Ah. Yes. Could you tell me anything about the witch – the enchantress, I mean – has she passed this way at all?'

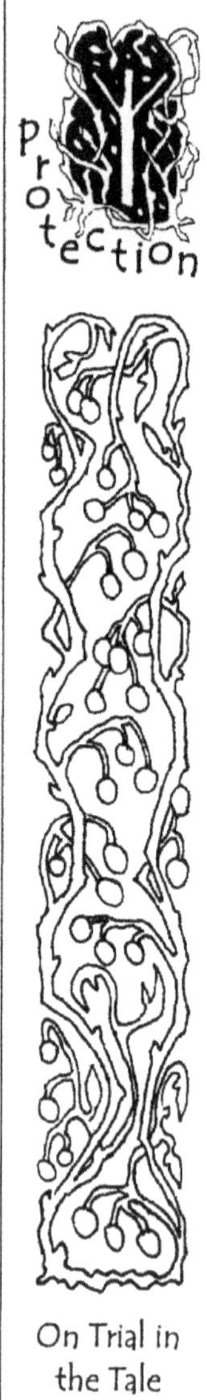

On Trial in
the Tale

'I can tell you many things,' said the oak. 'How long have you got?'

That didn't sound helpful.

'It's the witch I need to know about,' I said.

'Very well,' said the oak. 'But first, I'd like to tell you a story.'

I could see that getting information from trees was going to be a slow process.

'Very well,' I said. 'Fire away.'

The Oak's Tale –
The bird that preferred a cage

'Once upon a time,' said the oak-tree, 'a linnet was sitting in its cage by an open window. The bird's breezy song drifted distant on the spring air, and a wild far linnet heard it and came to perch on a nearby branch.

'You must be very unhappy, trapped in that cage,' said the wild bird. 'Look at me. I have my freedom. Would you like me to try to unlatch the cage and let you out?'

'I'm not sure,' said the pet bird. 'This is a spacious cage, and I have all the seed and water I could want. They bring me thistle heads,

you know, and nice green bunches of chickweed
from the kitchen-garden to pick over.'

'Oh,' said the wild bird. 'Chickweed! I do love
it.'

'Why don't you fly over to the kitchen-garden
and help yourself?' said the pet bird.

'I can't,' said the wild linnet. 'Not safe.
There's a cat...'

'So, I'm better off, chickweed-wise, than
you,' said the pet bird.

'Perhaps,' said the wildling, 'but wouldn't
you like to be out, flying free with us around the
gorse bushes? It's a fine life in the furze, you know.'

The pet bird thought about it a while.

'How old are you, cousin?'

'I have seen two summers. My mother
reached four – a fine age for a linnet,' said the wild
bird with pride.

'I have seen six summers,' said the cage bird,
'and still keeping very spry, thank you. Oh, and by
the way...'

'But you must want your freedom...'
interrupted the wild linnet.
Before it could finish there was a sinister swish of
wings, and the wild bird was gone.

'I was about to say,' the pet bird said to itself.
'Watch out for the sparrowhawk.'

'It's all about protection, you see,' said the
oak. 'Captivity might be worth it. Or you might
prefer dangerous freedom.'

*

While the tree was telling me this, my attention had wandered. I'm only a bird-brain after all. I couldn't help noticing another symbol, branded into the bark.

'What's this mark?' I asked.

'That's where she touched me. That enchantress. Went up in my branches for a while, horrid old baggage. And she left that mark.

'D'ye know what it means?' I asked.

'No idea,' said the oak. 'And that's not all, Yaffingale. Just look at what's grown on my trunk. That nasty-looking thing like raw liver, do you see?'

I did. Just like raw liver. Or a beefsteak.

'Did she do that to you? I asked, appalled.

'Think so,' said the oak. 'It wasn't there before.' And it fell silent.

I took a chance.

'If I tell you the meaning of the bark-mark, will you tell me more about the enchantress?'

'How would the likes of you know what it means?'

I took another chance.

'She has given me knowledge of the marks. You're not the only one who has them, you know. Yours means strength.'

'Pah!' said the oak. 'Anyone could have made that up!' But it seemed pleased.

'Now tell me about the witch, please.'

'Nothing to tell,' said the oak. 'She's gone to ground in my colleague up the hill. The lightning-struck one. She might still be there if you want her, though I don't know why you would. You beware of her, Master Yaffingale.'

I felt I wasn't much the wiser, but I thanked the oak anyway. What was I to make of all that story-telling?

I prepared to fly away.

'Juicy story, that,' said a voice.

'Pardon?' I said. 'Who said that?'

'Eh?' said the oak. It must be a bit deaf. I'm going crackers, I thought, hearing voices. That witch must have done something to my wits.

The Oak that broke

I should have given up and gone home there and then, but instead I went on to talk to the lightning-struck oak. It turned out to be very talkative.

'Heart of oak,' it said. 'Robust by name, robust by nature. My beams could have built a ship, you know. Or a house. Something solid and lasting. But I have had a change of heart.

It began with a lightning strike; a very sudden change for a tree. Our lives proceed slowly, bud by bud, twig by twig. No rushing about. Change takes time, or it usually does. But oh, the lightning. Oh, ouch. It was over in a flash, as these things are, but it changed me forever.

My poor heart was scorched and split, straight down the middle. And that was just the beginning. After a while, one of my heavy limbs turned and rolled over all the way to the ground. Not enough support, you see, with me being a bit broken. It left me lop-sided; not a pretty sight. And my heart began to break. Well, what can you expect? Troops of little fungi settled in, nibbling away. I didn't mind them, not really, but they softened my heart as they went. In the end it all became hollow.

'That was when that insufferable woman moved in. Witch, enchantress – call her what you like. Either way, she was a pain in the bark. Never stopped complaining.

My acorns were insufficiently nutritious, apparently; my butterflies, my beautiful purple emperors, clashed with her clothing; my branches were too crooked for comfortable sitting. And she moaned about the smell of burning still lingering. My trunk supported the wrong kind of lichens; my autumn colours were 'disappointing', if you please. The nerve of the woman. I'd have dropped one of my branches right on her head, if I'd had one conveniently ready. A nice heavy one.

'The demands she made! A more waterproof canopy; fire extinguishing equipment, in case of lightning striking twice; interior redecoration. Tenant's rights, she said. I pointed out that she'd moved in without so much as a by-your-leave, and wasn't paying any rent, either. She ignored me.

'Now, thank goodness, she's gone, moved on; but what do I find? She's carved something into my trunk. I can't see it, not having eyes, but I can feel the itching in the bark where she scratched it. I think she has killed me, Yaffingale.

It's a diabolical liberty, scribbling on people like that.'

I asked the broken oak if the enchantress had left a forwarding address, but it just grunted and said it was a tree not a post-office.

But I did know the meaning of the bark-mark she had left. It meant mortality. I thought it safest to keep my beak shut about that.

*

I hopped away from the lightning-struck oak. So much complaining, and no real useful information at all. You wouldn't think a big, tough tree could moan so much. And it still hadn't finished. The dreary complaints went on and on, and I moved off. Enough is enough. I hopped up onto the end of a fallen oak branch to scout out the surroundings.

'Ow,' said a voice. 'Get off!'

Not only were trees talking to me these days – their dead branches were, too. But I jumped off anyway. I found there was a horrid sticky stuff on my claws, and as soon as I touched the ground, the fallen leaves all glued themselves to my feet. It had come from the oak branch, leaking out in pearly drops. I'd never seen anything like it. But a second look told me it wasn't a branch at all. It was a toadstool, its cap marked with rings, just like a cut branch. I had broken it, and the cap was bleeding this sticky milk.

I scuffled about on the floor, trying to dislodge all the leaves.

'Serve you right,' said the voice. 'By the way, she's gone to the beech grove.'

Yaffingale – Double Agent at Work

You can imagine how confused I felt by all this. Looking back, I can see I should have worked out what was going on far sooner. But I was young and callow then and took things at face value. A very green woodpecker indeed, I was. Not only that, but I had got myself into a very uncomfortable position indeed, acting as a double agent between the witch and the elder-tree. If I'd had any sense, I would have flown off and found myself another forest, but I was too inexperienced to see how dangerous it was. Anyway, let me go on with the story.

I came away from the broken oak and decided it was time to report back to the elder.

'You've taken your time, where have you been?' said the elder. 'And whatever's the matter with your feet, Yaffingale?'

'I got stuck,' I said, in answer to both questions, still trying to unglue the leaves from my feet.

'Hmm,' said the elder, 'Not very efficient. What news of the enchantress, eh?'

'Haven't seen much of her, but the oaks have,' I said.

And what do they say?' The elder's tone suggested it was speaking to an idiot, which was probably true at the time.

I recounted the sound oak's story of the linnets. The elder showed no interest at all, so I told it what the lightning-struck tree had said.

'Ha!' said the elder, making me jump. 'D'ye think that tree's a reliable witness, Yaffingale?' I shrugged. At least I had the sense not to offer opinions.

'It's certainly bad-tempered,' I said, 'and glad to see the back of her too. She was a terrible tenant.'

'Hmm,' said the elder. 'Anything else?'

I was unsure whether I should mention the weird meaty fungus that had appeared. I hesitated just a moment too long.

'Anything growing on those oaks?' It was clear the elder knew more than it was letting on.

I decided honesty was the best policy when asked a direct question.

'The oak complained – the sound one, that is – of a fungus.'

'Hmm,' said the elder, very non-committal, 'makes sense.'

I decided to leave out the part about the voices I was hearing. I kept quiet about the marks I'd seen on the trees, too.

'The enchantress has gone to the beech grove,' I said.

The elder was pleased at that.

'Good work, Yaffingale. Now off you go, follow in her wake, talk to the beeches, see what she's up to, and report back to me.'

Looking back, it was a thoroughly thankless task, but youngsters do like a bit of adventure, don't they, so I carried on. I took a day or two off for a rest and to get the pesky leaves off my feet. I could scarcely fly straight with all that rubbish weighing me down. I'd already done a crash landing on an anthill, I'm embarrassed to relate. I'd have sworn the ants were laughing at me. I stopped to do a bit of idle wood pecking, too, as you do, but then set off for the beech grove in search of the enchantress as the elder had instructed.

'She went that way,' said a chorus of little voices.

'Thank you,' I said. 'Oi, who said that?'

Troops of little fungi were forming proper trails across the forest floor, and I had the distinct feeling they were doing the talking. But toadstools can't talk, can they?

This is a strange story altogether, you will have noticed, and I'm sure you will be wondering why I didn't make a run for it. You must have known you were imperilled, Yaffingale, you will be saying. The truth is, I discounted the peril, overlooked it. I felt special, singled out by the attentions of the witch and the magical elder tree. Oh, how I gambled with my life for that attention. Stupid, then, you will say. Yes, but I was enjoying myself.

*

I caught up with the enchantress at
the beech grove, but kept my
distance. It was odd, I thought, the
way she would pause in the darkest
shades, stepping delicately to avoid
the spots of flickering light that
elbowed their way through the
falling leaves. Or was the light
flickering to avoid her? She had
better hurry up, I thought, if she
doesn't care for the light. The
foliage is thinning day by day.

She had the place to herself,
though; moles upended, squirrels
scattered, voles vanished, shrews
shrunk away. Roebucks snorted
and took a different way home.
Every sensible creature kept out of
her way. Except me. She knew I was
there, of course, but it was a while
before she acknowledged me.

'Ho, Yaffingale,' she said. I couldn't tell
whether she was about to converse with me or hurl
a thunderbolt.

'Good morning, Madame,' I said, very wary,
and ready to dodge behind a trunk if she turned
nasty.

'The elder sent you, hmm?'

'Yes, Madame. I reported back, told it the
story the oak tree told me. Would you like to hear
it?'

'No,' she said. 'I know all those tales. Good grief, I wrote one or two of them myself.' I didn't know whether to believe that, but at least it was something to tell the elder next time. 'What else?'

'The elder enquired about a fungus growing on the oak. I said I had seen it.'

I carefully left out the part about the voices. Who could tell if that would please her or not?

She turned on me suddenly and glared.

'How did you know to find me here in the beech grove?'

'The shattered oak told me you were heading this way.' I hoped this was an acceptable answer, even though it was untrue. I was not about to admit having taken directions from a squashed toadstool.

'Hmm,' she said. 'Keep me informed, Yaffingale.' And off she went, dodging the dapples of light in the beech grove, a grey presence among the bright brown and yellow falling leaves. I watched her awhile, working her way from trunk to trunk, leaving her mark on each one. She was a terror for graffiti, that enchantress.

*

I have some experience of trees; they are my life's work, after all, and my living. I can see her now, winding herself round a trunk, squinting, extending a pale thumb to brand the tree, a little waft of steam rising from her touch. The trees looked glad to see the back of her when she moved on. She marked them all, though. Very thorough.

I returned to the elder.

'Something new?' it asked, evidently surprised to see me.

'The enchantress told me she wrote some of the trees' stories herself,' I said. 'Just thought you ought to know.'

The elder wasn't interested.

'Follow her, interrogate the beech-tree,.' it said.

The Beech

Inspired by the beech-tree (Fagus sylvatica) a tall, beautiful forest tree that creates deep shade in the summertime and a depth of fallen leaves in the winter. It is associated with many fungi including the porcelain fungus (Oudemansiella mucida) which has a slight glow-in-the-dark capability and the striking black and white magpie inkcap (Coprinopsis picacea).

When I got back to the beech grove, she was gone. I'd given her plenty of time to finish what she was doing. I didn't want her to catch me talking to the trees. I chose the largest, oldest, most sensible-looking beech-tree. The enchantress' mark was on its trunk, sure enough.

I tapped on the bark.

'Wake up,' I said. 'Tell me about the witch.'

'Eh?' said the beech tree. I tapped again, harder.

'The witch,' I said. 'What news?'

'I am a beautiful tree,' said the beech, apparently answering a completely different question.

I was taken by surprise. 'Why do you think you're beautiful?' I asked.

'My bark. My beautiful, smooth, grey-green bark, trimmed with emerald mosses,' said the beech.

Trust me to find one that had gone all poetic.

'Very fine,' I said, 'now, about the witch...'

'And then, there are my beautiful leaves,' said the beech, ignoring me. 'My great wealth of gorgeous, crinkly-edged, graceful leaves, the brightest, freshest green to be seen in spring...'

I feared the tree was about to collapse into rhyming couplets.

'And now I say my fond farewell,
As they flutter dying to the soil...'

Not even a proper rhyme. I couldn't stand any more of it.

'Wouldn't you rather tell me a story about the witch?' I didn't have all day to spend on poetry appreciation.

'You don't waste words, do you?' said the beech tree. 'Rude. Very rude. Not so much as a good morning and you go straight into making demands. I'll tell you what I'll do, Master Yaffingale...'

'You'll tell me your own story?' I could see there was no short-cut to getting the information I wanted, so I sighed and settled down to preen my feathers. 'Go on, then, time's wasting.'

'Hmm,' said the beech tree, 'well, this is an old story...'

'They always are,' I said, trying not to look bored.

'Will you stop interrupting, Master Yaffingale? Pay attention; you might learn something. And don't go pecking my beautiful bark. I don't want it spoiled.'

'Can we get on?' I said.

The Beech's Tale – Worms' Rights

'Once upon a time,' said the beech-tree, 'a thrush and a blackbird had got hold of a worm, one each end.'

'It's mine, I'm entitled to it,' said the thrush.

'No, it isn't. I saw it first. It's my right to have it,' said the blackbird.

'Oi!' said worm. 'What about my rights?'

'You keep out of this,' said the thrush.

'That's right,' said the blackbird. 'None of your business.'

'I think it's very much my business,' said the worm, 'when one of you has me by the head, and one by the tail.'

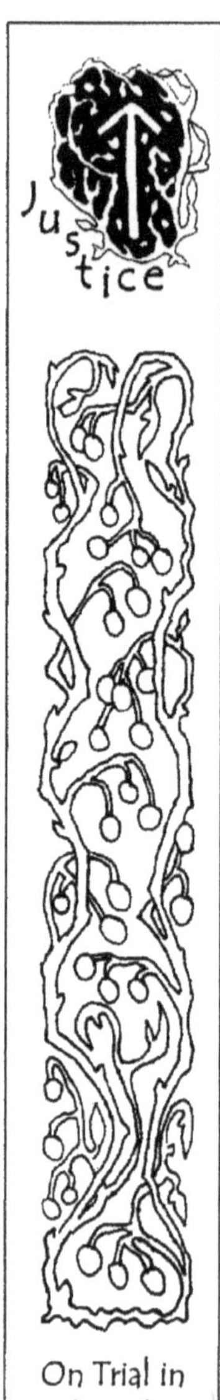

On Trial in
the Tale

'I've got the head end,' said the thrush, 'so the whole worm is mine by rights.'

'Oh, no you don't!' said the blackbird. 'Anyone can see I have the head end. The worm belongs to me.'

'Do you mind?' said the worm. 'Both ends belong to me, actually. So, if you'll kindly both stop pulling, and let go, I'd be much obliged.'

'The birds were so confused by their dinner answering back that they both let go, and while they fought each other, the worm made itself scarce and got on with its useful job of digesting things in the soil. But the young thrushes and blackbirds in their nests went hungry for want of that nice juicy worm, and none of them thrived.'

That was the tale. But then, the tree said, 'Answer me this, was justice done, Master Yaffingale: who was within their rights? Was it the thrush, the blackbird or the worm?'

Why do these trees think I have the answers to their philosophical conundrums?

I was going to point out that if I'm on an
anthill enjoying a few ants for lunch, I don't waste
much time discussing ants' rights. But I felt that
didn't answer the question, so I said nothing.
Played dumb.

'Not difficult, for you,' observed the beech-
tree as if it had read my mind. 'Now I haven't
mentioned my beautiful boughs, have I? I have a
wealth of beauty, you know.'

I really couldn't let it get back to quoting
poetry, so I distracted it by pointing out the mark
on its trunk.

'She has disfigured my beauty,' said the
beech.

'Now about my branches...'

'I can tell you its meaning,' I said. I really
could. 'If you tell me about the witch.'

'Go on then,' said the beech.

'It means wealth.'

'I just used that very word myself!' said the
beech, unimpressed. 'Now about my
crown...'

A very determined talker,
that tree, so I interrupted.

'Do you know about the
fungi?'

'What fungi?'

I indicated toward the
deathly-pale, porcelain thin
mushrooms that were
sprouting out of its trunk.

'Oh!' said the beech. 'My beautiful smooth trunk disfigured even more! That witch...'

'Have you got a light?' said the porcelain fungus, as I hopped away. 'I have.' And it had, too; in the dim light of the

beech grove, it was glowing. 'I think she was headed for the birches, by the way.'

*

As I left the beeches I heard a voice, or should I say a sobbing. Down among the leaf-litter there were stout black-and-white toadstools, and all of them were crying. Black tears were seeping out of their caps and leaving inky trails down the stems. Some of them had wept away their whole caps and were nothing but a stained stalk. Very strange, and quite affecting.

'Why are you crying?' I asked.

The only answer was a fresh outburst of inky tears as they dissolved in their own misery.

*

I flew back to the elder tree to make my report.

'You're late,' it said. Very rude. But then a magical being can afford to be rude if it likes.

'Well,' said the tree. 'What can you tell me?'

'She's been in the beech grove, causing havoc. I spoke to the biggest beech, and it told me a story.' I didn't bother mentioning poetry, in case it gave the elder ideas. Instead, I rattled through the tale of worms' rights.

'Barking mad,' observed the elder, unimpressed. 'Is that all?'

'Yes,' I said. 'That's all.' Though it wasn't.

'Are you sure?' Had I been caught lying?

I tried for a nonchalant tone.

'Oh, well, it did mention the fungi that had appeared on its trunk. Glow-in-the-dark, apparently.' That was partially true.

'That makes sense,' said the elder-tree, satisfied.

I had no idea why it made sense, to tell the truth. But at least the elder had stopped asking awkward questions.

'She's gone to the birches,' I said and flew off without waiting for an answer.

A clump of glistening toadstools on a stump sang to me, 'She went that way!' Lovely four-part harmony, I have to say.

'Thanks,' I said. I was getting used to being engaged in conversation by fungi now.

38

The Birch

Inspired by the silver birch (Betula pendula) a graceful tree, often the first to colonise new ground. It is associated with many fungi, including the birch bolete (Leccinum scabrum), an elegant toadstool of late summer and early autumn.

The birch trees, when I reached them were – there is no other word – beautiful. So very many trees in the grove, too, their shapely yellow leaves were falling, making soft patterns against the white trunks. A sort of elegant yellow rain. Even I was impressed, though my opinion of trees has gone downhill lately. I headed for the largest, oldest tree in the hope that it might have something sensible to say. It certainly had the witch's mark – they all did. But as I got nearer, I could hear it moaning.

'Oh, woe, woe!'

Oh, no, no, I thought. A miserable one. Was it too late to choose another?

'Yaffingale,' it said, 'come and sit with me.'

Definitely too late.

I moved nearer.

'Good afternoon,' I said. Politeness never does any harm.

'What's good about it?' said the birch-tree. 'What's good about any afternoon?'

I couldn't think of a helpful answer, so I plunged straight in.

'Have you seen the witch, the enchantress?'

'Don't talk to me about her,' said the birch, 'look at the horrid mark she's left on my trunk.'

Indeed, the enchantress had left her stamp on the trunk.

'Is that why you're unhappy?' I asked.

'I'm always unhappy,' said the birch, dropping a few more sad leaves. 'It's in my nature, you know.'

I could see this was going to be a very unjolly interview.

'I'm sure you've suffered great misfortunes,' I said. I sincerely hoped it wasn't going to list them all for me.

'Misfortunes!' wailed the birch. 'Look at me – see how my twigs droop earthwards. They are weighted down with ancient sorrows.'

'But your beautiful white bark...' I said, hoping to cheer it up.

'Used to be lovely dark bark,' said the birch. 'Turned white with anguish. It is the badge of my sorrows. If your feathers had turned white with worry, Yaffingale, would you regard them as beautiful?'

There was no answer to that.

But I did wonder how such a beautiful living thing as a birch-tree could be such a complete and utter misery. I certainly wasn't going to ask it.

'I suppose you'd like to tell me a story,' I said, resigned. It seemed the only way forward.

'I am a short-lived tree,' the birch told me, 'So let us make this a short story.'

I was tempted to retort that it was not as short-lived as a woodpecker, and could it be made shorter still. But there's no telling these trees anything, is there?

The Birch's Story –
The deer that loved wolves

'Once upon a time,' said the birch-tree, 'a man saw a deer being chased by a pack of wolves. He was so shocked by the terror of the deer as it ran, and the mercilessness of the wolves when they brought it down, that it gave him an idea. He decided to build a tall wall all around the forest where the deer lived to keep the wolves out. The deer were grateful, and thanked him for making them safe.

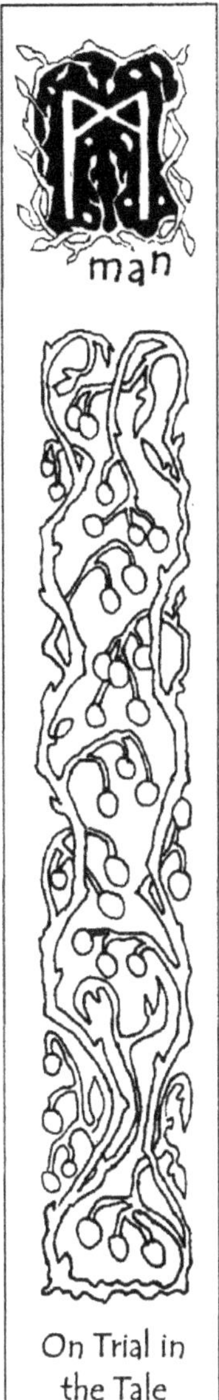

On Trial in
the Tale

41

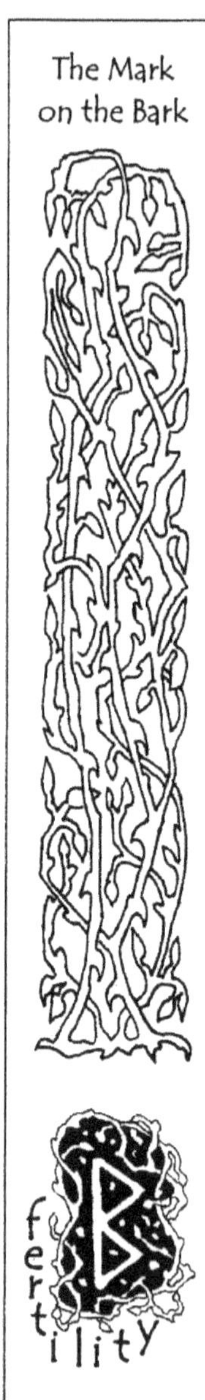

The herd thrived and grew, and the young, the old and the sick were all protected from the wolves, just as the man intended. He left them alone for a long time, but one day he decided to go and see how they did.

'Oh, my goodness! The herd was large, but many of them were old and sick, and all of them were starving. They had eaten every leaf and shoot, and even the bark off the trees as far up as they could reach. The trees were all dying, and the woodland was devastated.

An ancient stag limped up and begged the man to take down the wall.

'There is not enough food for all these young and all the old and sick. We need the wolves to keep our numbers in check so we may have a healthy herd. Please let the wolves back in, sir. They may be cruel, but we love them and when they come, they may begin with me." And the old stag limped painfully away.

The man was very sad, as he had only meant to help.'

It had been too much to hope for a happy ending, I knew.

'But he took down the wall, didn't he?' I asked.

'He did,' said the birch, weeping more leaves. 'Absolute carnage for a while after the wolves got back in. Long time before the balance was restored. Should the man have put up the wall in the first place? Road to hell is paved with good intentions...'

It lapsed into miserable silence.

'If I tell you the meaning of your bark-mark, will you tell me where the witch has gone?'

'I already know,' said the birch, 'it means misery.'

'Well, that's where you'd be wrong. It means fertility. You and your kind are fertile trees. Is not that something to celebrate?'

'Oh,' said the birch, 'wonderful! Even more of us to be miserable!'

I demanded news of the witch in return.

The birch-tree grudgingly told me that the toadstools that sprang up after the witch passed through had a very odd effect.

'You wouldn't believe it, Master Yaffingale, but I could sense the other birch trees in the forest. I could sense the toadstools, too. And I think we may be magically connected now. Strange isn't it?'

The birch could be bonkers, of course. But if not, this is surely valuable information. Too valuable to give away to the elder, or the enchantress, for nothing.

As I left, I heard another voice. I was getting used to it by now.

'She's gone to the yew-tree,' said a toadstool with a shaggy stem and a posh voice. 'Best of luck getting much sense out of that one. Thinks it knows everything.'

The Yew

Inspired by the yew-tree (Taxus baccata) a heavy-set evergreen capable of living to a great age. Various fungi grow on or with it, including the sulphur-yellow chicken of the woods (Laetiporus sulphureus).

The yew-tree, when I visited it, had the witch's mark quite clear on its trunk.

It started talking before I could get a word in.

'Let me tell you about myself,' said the yew-tree. 'If nothing else, I'm a stable feature of the landscape. Old, certainly. Jaded? Well, sometimes. But as the saying goes, it's no good getting old if you don't get crafty. I have wisdom, too. You learn a great deal if you just sit and watch down the centuries. And you will have noticed, Yaffingale, that I keep my leaves all the year round – none of that flighty changing of clothes every few seasons. I change mine when they need it and not before. Much more dignified. I can protect myself, too. Any leaf-thief that tries to make off with my foliage will live to regret it. Or, rather, not live. I have poisons, you know.'

'I will not touch your foliage, Master Yew-tree,' I said hastily.

'That's Mistress Yew-tree, if you don't mind. I am a female tree, and don't you forget it, or I'll breathe something noxious at you.'

'Absolutely I will not forget,' I said, hopping backwards. 'No offence intended, madam, I'm sure.'

'Why exactly are you here, Yaffingale?' asked the yew.

'Well,' I said, 'You are a tree of great knowledge and wisdom...'

'Never mind the buttering-up,' said the yew. 'Get on with it.'

You'd think an ancient tree would have more patience. As if it didn't have all the time in the world, after all.

'I know what you're thinking,' said the yew. 'You're thinking I have all the time in the world, aren't you?'

That was very unnerving. Could a tree possibly read a bird's mind? Or was it just a clever guess? I hoped so, or I was in trouble.

'Never crossed my mind, madam,' I said, all innocence. 'But I did wonder if you have any news of the witch – the enchantress, I mean. Has she passed by at all?'

I knew she had by the mark on the yew's trunk, but it seemed impolite to point it out.

'She has,' said the tree grumpily, 'but before I say any more about her, I would wish to...'

'Tell me a story, I know,' I said, resigned. 'Every tree tells me a story.'

'Hmm,' said the yew and settled herself in a miasma of ill-temper as she gathered her thoughts.

The Yew's Tale – The lizards that owned all the world

'Once upon a time there was – but no, let me ask you a question first, Yaffingale. You believe, do you not, that you and your kind will be living here in this forest forever?'

That was an odd question.

'I'd like to think so,' I said warily.

'No doubt you would,' said the yew-tree. 'But there are no certainties in the world, you know. I'll get back to the story. Once upon a time, great lizards roamed the earth.'

'Nonsense,' I said. I just couldn't help myself.

'It's a story, stupid. Shut your beak and listen. Now where was I? Oh, yes, these lizards thought they were so big and so clever that the world was all their own, for ever and ever.

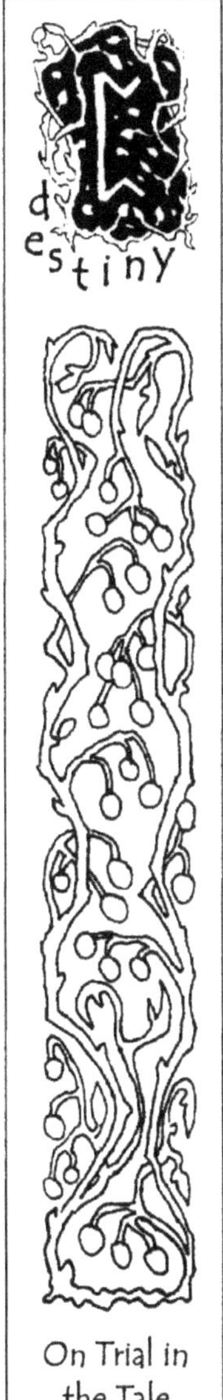

On Trial in
the Tale

47

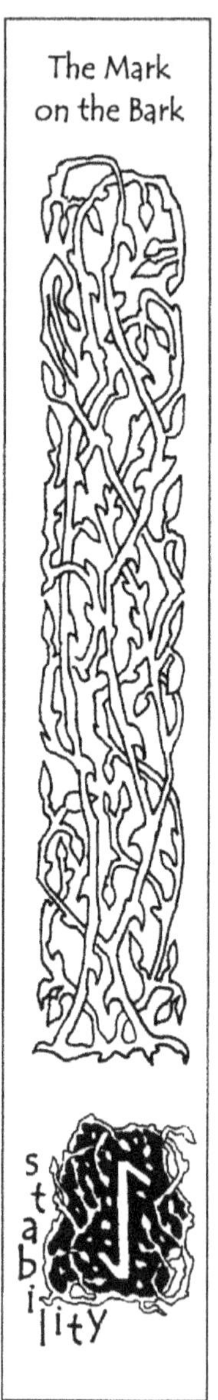

But they were wrong. What do you think happened?'

'They weren't so clever as they thought?' I guessed.

'Partly right,' said the yew-tree. 'Bigger, cleverer lizards – some as big as trees - came along and took over the place. The smaller, stupider lizards were very affronted and said, 'How dare you invade us! This is our world! We are entitled to it!"

'So, what happened?' I asked.

'The bigger, cleverer lizards ate them.'

'That is very shocking,' I said, though I wasn't entirely surprised.

'No doubt,' said the yew-tree, 'but it stopped them bleating about entitlements.'

I still didn't quite see the point of the story, but that horrid old yew-tree read my mind again.

'The point being, Yaffingale, that destiny is destiny, and it isn't always kind; the world is always changing, nothing is forever, and nature doesn't care a fig for entitlements.'

'I see,' I said, though I wasn't sure I did.

An unpleasant thought struck me.

'I say, there aren't any of those giant lizards still lurking about, are there?' The thought of a tree-sized lizard crashing about in the forest was unsettling.

'No,' said the yew-tree. 'They all died out, too, long ago, and their old bones lie in the ground beneath us.'

'Not so clever as they thought, then.'

'No-one ever is, Yaffingale.'

I thought the whole story very far-fetched, but I wasn't going to argue it out.

'Very enlightening, Mistress Yew-tree, I'm sure. But now will you tell me about the witch – the enchantress?'

'Oh, her. She wandered up to me, put her nasty bony fingers on my bark.'

'Yes,' I said. 'If I tell you the meaning of the bark-mark, will you tell me where she went.'

'Astonish me,' said the yew-tree.

'Your mark indicates stability.' And so it did.

'Hmm,' said the yew-tree, unimpressed. 'Pretty obvious. But that's not all, just look – this excrescence appeared.' She meant the hideous yellow fungus on her trunk. 'And I feel it will be the death of me, in time. Nothing lasts for ever, not even ancient me. You keep away from her, Yaffingale, or you'll have toadstools sprouting out of your tail-feathers. She's with the ash-trees now, I understand.'

*

49

Butter yellow it was, the fungus growing on the yew. Not a colour you see all that often round here. With a touch of orange, and quite shapeless. The enchantress must have lost her sense of style. Or her mind. But there it was, bursting out of the dark trunk in the dark shades under the boughs. A very unholy colour, if you ask me. I thought the witch must have gone inside the tree and shovelled this thing out through a knot-hole. The yew looked horrified, being saddled with this crime against good taste, but I don't think it had any say in the matter, to be honest. I did feel sorry for the tree. Of all the things the enchantress left behind her, this was the worst so far. The elder got its own ears, after all; the beech tree got its own lighting system; the poor yew is wearing a fashion disaster. Very unkind of the witch to do that. She must really have hated the yew.

I was turning to leave when a voice said,
'Cluck!' It was the yellow fungus.
'Pardon?' I said.
'Cluck, cluck!'
I flew away. Anyone who thinks I'm going to hold a conversation with a fungus that thinks it's a chicken is sadly mistaken.

The Ash

Inspired by the ash-tree (Fraxinus excelsior) a tree with much ancient folk-lore attached to it, and sometimes called the Tree of Life. A burnt-looking fungus called King Alfred's cakes (Daldinia concentrica) often grows on dead branches.

In the ash-grove I found all the trees wearing the mark of the enchantress, so I chose one at random, and asked for news.

'Some say I am the most beautiful of trees,' said the ash, 'a true goddess of the woods. I say piffle. I am a careful tree, first of all. You will have noticed that I keep my buds closed long after other trees have put out their spring leaves. I take my time. This means I miss the benefit of the early sunshine, but, oh, I am never frost-nipped. It's my choice, Master Yaffingale. Works for me.

'My heritage goes far back, right back to the very first ash-tree, my ancient ancestor. That tree bore bunches of keys on its boughs. Each key carried a seed. Each seed carried the essence of something important, as well as the makings of another tree.

When the seeds grew, each founded a line of trees.

My own line carries the keys of knowledge. As you can see, Master Yaffingale, my keys are ripe and ready to fall, and spread knowledge.'

'Then you must know everything,' I said. 'Tree of knowledge you are for sure.'

'I do,' said the ash-tree. 'I know everything. But I understand none of it. The key to wisdom, you see, grows on another tree. Knowledge without wisdom is pretty useless stuff, you know. I am burdened with all this information – it's why my branches are curved, buckled by the weight of it all. And no way to make any sense of it. I'll tell you a story now.'

'I thought you just had.'

'Just telling you about myself. This is the real story.'

The Ash's Tale –
The tree that climbed up and down

The ash-tree clacked its branches and settled down to speak.

'I shall tell you the tale of a distant relative of mine,' it said, very pompous. 'We are a superior sort of tree, ashes, so I assume it is entirely true. It is a matter of nomenclature.'

It sounded very dull, and I prepared to let my attention wander.

'However,' said the ash-tree, 'it is also a great adventure.'

I perked up again.

'Once upon a time, an ash-tree wanted to see the whole world. Other trees said this was quite impossible. A tree's world was limited to its immediate surroundings, and that was that. But this ash-tree was determined. It tore its roots out of the ground and stumped off through the forest. After a while it saw a mountain in the distance. That was clearly the place to go. You could surely see the whole world from the top of that. So, the ash-tree stumbled and climbed until it reached the mountain-top. The view was remarkable, and the tree was pleased with itself for being so adventurous.

'Here I am,' it said. 'And now I shall call myself a mountain-ash to distinguish myself from the common ashes below. I've earned it.'

'Oh, no you won't,' said a voice. It was a rowan-tree growing nearby. 'That name is already taken. It is another name for me.'

'But rowan-tree, you're not even an ash at all. Not any sort of ash. You're a sort of rose relative. How can you lay claim to the name mountain-ash?'

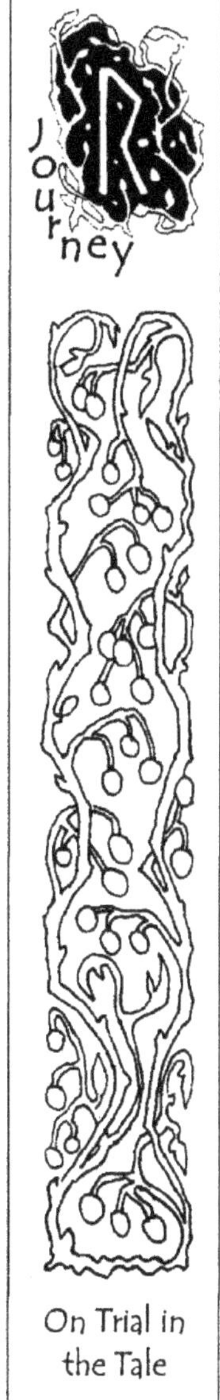

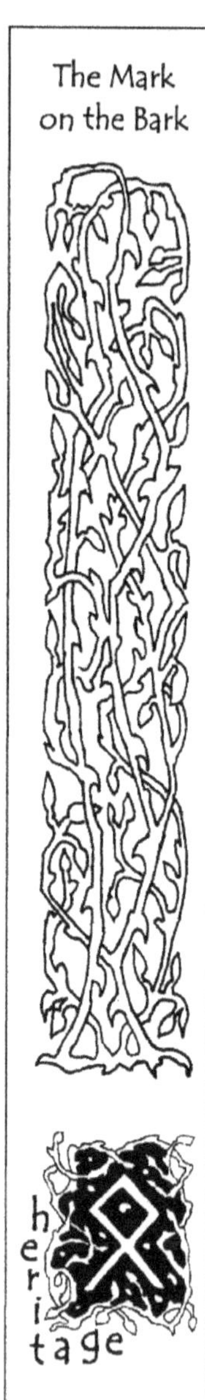

'It's a figure of speech,' said the rowan. 'My leaves are somewhat like yours. There's a resemblance, you know. Anyway, I'm the mountain-ash round here. It's my name and I'm keeping it. You're just a common ash.'

'How many names do you need?' asked the ash, more than a little miffed. 'And don't call me common.'

'The rowan declined to answer, and the ash-tree stumped off again back down the mountain, thinking its remarkable journey had been a waste of time. Had it? I don't know. I haven't tried it myself. But when that tree got home and settled itself back in the soil, it told the other ashes of its humiliation by the rowan. And ever since then, we have adopted extra names for ourselves. None of your dead-common names, of course – we prefer something more poetic. My particular favourite is The Venus of the Woods. Pleasingly high-class, don't you think?'

Well, I'd never heard anyone call ashes anything so pretentious. I still haven't. But I wasn't bothered about that at the time.

'I've heard your story, ash-tree,' I said. 'Now, about the witch...'

The ash-tree fell into a grumpy silence. I waited a while, and then said, 'Well, you must know whether the witch – the enchantress - passed by, even if you don't understand what she was up to.'

'Oh, her,' said the ash-tree. 'Yes, she was here. I thought to ask her if she could bring me wisdom – it's all I want – but she isn't trustworthy. Throws thunderbolts if she thinks you're being cheeky. Very bad news for a tree, thunderbolts. So I kept quiet. Much good my discretion did me, Yaffingale. Look what appeared, after she passed by.'

'Yes, yes,' I was running out of patience. 'If I tell you the meaning of the mark, will you tell me about the witch? It means heritage.' And so it did.

'Hmm,' said the ash. 'I used that very word myself, didn't I? But she also left strange growths on my dead wood. They look like cakes left too long in the oven. Burned black. What do you think, Yaffingale? Can you smell burning?'

'No,' I said. 'But your trunk is a smooth, pale grey; they are black. Black and grey is a very chic colour combination. Rather smart.'

'Ha!' said the ash-tree. 'You're not as stupid as you look, are you? Clever answer, Master Yaffingale. Since I can't be rid of them, I'll try to think of them as chic.'

'Ashes to ashes,' said a chorus of little voices. 'She's at the elm-grove.'

The burned-looking fungi were giving directions. So I set off.

The Elm

Inspired by the English Elm (Ulmus procera) a beautiful tree, once common in the English landscape, but now devastated by an unfriendly fungus. A parasitic fungus that used to appear commonly on elm-trunks is the dryad's saddle (Cerioporus squamosus).

Among the elms, I saw they all bore the witch's mark, so I chose one. I always thought the elm was a gloomy tree, but this one reached new heights of misery. Not so much a tale, this one, more of a prophecy. And a pretty unpleasant one, too.

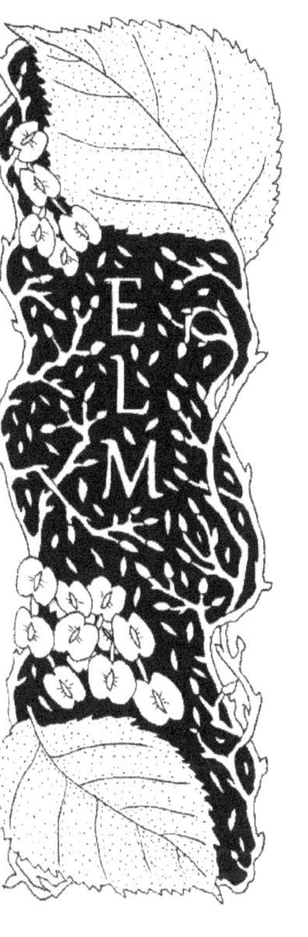

'This is a tale of woe, Master Yaffle,' the elm-tree said. There's a surprise, I thought, but it was best not to interrupt. The sooner this tree got started, the sooner it'd finish, and I could be on my way.

'Woe, woe and woe, again,' said the elm. Honestly, was there ever a more woeful tree?

'Why are you so woeful, elm-tree?' I just couldn't help asking.

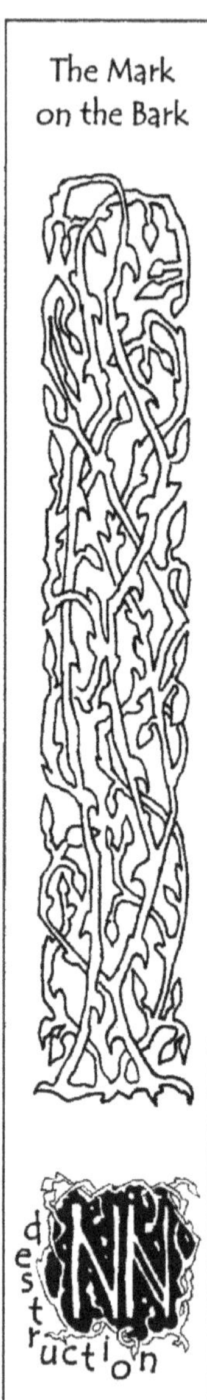

'I'll tell you,' said the elm, dropping a batch of mournful leaves. 'One day, far ahead in the not-happened-yet, there will come a great plague. Every elm in the land will fall sick. Many will die, and those that don't will be cut to the ground and grow only as scrubby shrubs. A terrible future for a tall, proud tree. Dead or stunted, every one of us.'

'Is that it?' I asked, surprised at such a short tale. Still, it was a horrid prophecy if you happen to be an elm. 'I suppose this plague won't affect woodpeckers?' I added.

'Only in that there will be a lot less wood for you to peck,' said the elm, moping again. This time, I did not offer to translate the bark-mark. I could read it perfectly well, and it said destruction.

I asked the elm if it had seen the enchantress.

'Oh, her,' said the elm tree. 'Yes, she passed by. Kicked me in the trunk as she went. Spiteful. And look what's grown, right where her boot touched me.'

Sure enough, a brown scaly thing was growing straight out of the trunk.

I hopped on to it – unpleasantly spongy under my claws, I must say – and had a peck at it. Very sour taste. I passed a few more woeful pleasantries with the elm and was happy to depart.

Part Three
Between Trunk and Thunderbolt

Telling Tales

I flew back to the elder-tree and recounted the tales the trees had told me.

'So there you are, your honour, that's as much as I can tell you.'

This wasn't strictly true, as the elm also said something else; she was able to share her woeful predictions with other elms, she said, and other trees, too, since the toadstools appeared. They came with the enchantress, too, apparently. I wasn't telling the elder-tree that. It pays to keep something back, I find.

*

I thought I'd better check in with the witch, too, so I asked a toadstool, as you do, where I might find her.

'She's back in the beeches,' it squeaked. So off I went.

At the moment I arrived, the sky darkened. I'd had no idea that enchantress could do things like that, and it was ominous to say the least. She came crashing down out of the trees, ragged and furious.

Her cloak snagged on a branch, and she shouted such a curse that half the tree split open. There was another curse as she freed herself, and there she was, hovering in front of me, feet off the ground, and everything darkening around her. There was no doubt it was me she wanted.

'You have been... duplicitous,' she howled.

I didn't know what duplicitous meant, not then, but it certainly wasn't good. Still, she was waiting for an answer.

'Madame,' I said, making myself as small as I could to form a less tempting target in case she started with the thunderbolts.

'Don't you madame me,' she said, 'you two-faced, double-dealing, deceitful, lying toad.'

'I'm sure I never told you any untruths, Madame,' I said. That was a fact.

'It's not what you said, Yaffingale, it's what you didn't say. What you deliberately left out. You kept me in the dark.'

I wanted to point out that it was she who was keeping me in the dark, just at that moment. The whole forest had taken on a night-time aspect. I could hear confused owls in the distance. The enchantress herself was only visible by her eyes glowing green.

'I did?'

'That beastly elder-tree stole some of my magical powers. You know all about it.'

'I do?' It was news to me. 'No, I don't. All I've done is tell the trees' stories to the elder. Nothing else. It shared no secrets with me.'

She was not appeased, not the least bit.

'The elder has stolen my powers and it's all your fault!'

I really didn't see how it was my fault, but I didn't have time to stop and think about it, because this time she really did throw a thunderbolt. I dodged out of the way, and it hit the beech tree behind me which gave a terrible echoing groan.

'Sorry,' I said to it, and flew off as fast as I could. She followed, and she'd have caught me too, had she not snagged her cloak on another tree and given me a head start. I could hear her cursing and crashing about the beech grove, but I didn't look back. I fled straight to the elder-tree in the hope that it might protect me. But another shock awaited me there.

'You used me!' I cried.

'Oh, come now,' said the elder, 'you enjoyed it.'

'Well,' I admitted, 'I suppose I did, up to a point?'

'What point?'

'The point where she tried to blow my head off.'

'Ah,' said the elder. 'Unfortunate, that.'

'More unfortunate for the beech-tree she hit by mistake.'

I zipped round to the sheltered side of the elder's meagre trunk and tried to look inconspicuous. On the way, I thought I caught sight of another bark-mark, a new one.

Did that mean deception? Or was it just a bit of flaking bark? I didn't have time to puzzle it out.

'Now then,' said the elder-tree. 'What do you think?' Was this a rhetorical question, I wondered, or did it require an answer.

'What do you think, Yaffingale, about the trees?'

'Pardon?'

'Tell me what you think,' said the elder again, speaking as if to an idiot. 'What d'ye think of the oak, for instance?'

'Oh,' I said, 'I see. Well, it's strong, but temperamental. Likes to complain.'

'Hmm,' said the elder. 'And the beech-tree? What d'ye think of that?'

'Vain,' I said. 'Give it a looking glass and it'd admire itself all day long.'

'Good,' said the elder, 'we're making progress. What of the birch?'

'Sad,' I said. 'Proper misery. Sees the worst in everything.'

'Very depressing company for you, I'm sure,' said the elder. 'What about the ash?'

'Pompous,' I said. 'High opinion of itself. Quite undeserved, if you ask me.'

'And the yew-tree?'

I thought a while about that.

'I suppose it's very stable,' I said, doubtfully.

'Yes, stability. Oldest tree in the forest, that sort of thing. Thinks it knows everything.'

'And the elm-tree?'

'Gloomy,' I said. 'Spends its time foretelling disasters. Proper little doom-monger.'

'So, in general,' the elder-tree summed up, 'they're self-centred or miserable or both. Am I right?'

'I think they enjoy it,' I said. 'They seem quite happy as long as they're got something to complain about.'

'As I expected,' said the elder. 'Now tell me what you think about me. The truth, mind.'

I hadn't expected to be put on the spot like that, and fell silent.

'Come along now,' said the elder. 'Such silence! And you so talkative, too.'

I pulled myself together.

'Oh. Well. Magical, of course. You are a magical tree, your honour, and not in the least grumpy with it.'

'Flattering,' said the elder, 'but not what you really think, is it? What do you really think, Yaffingale?'

I had the feeling, not for the first time that the tree could read my thoughts. What I really thought was that it was sly, cunning, crafty and unreliable, and that I didn't think it had my best interests at heart. But I could hardly say so. I struggled to find another flattering fib, but before I could invent one, something quite shocking happened. Out of the sky came the enchantress again, crashing through the branches, trailing darkness.

'Got you,' she said, all malevolence. I opened one eye. She was definitely talking to me. This time the thunderbolt would not miss. Point-blank range, after all. I squeezed my eyes shut, shaking. And then, well, something even more shocking happened.

I was picked up, spun and crushed, squashed into a most unnatural shape. I opened an eye and could still see the enchantress dancing about in a ragged fury, but it was a while before I understood I was inside the elder-tree, squeezed into its thin trunk.

'Let me out!'

'Not safe,' said the elder right in my ear, uncomfortably close. I'd have jumped out of my skin if I'd had room. I squirmed in the confined space. I could see now why the enchantress had been so glad to get out. It was very uncomfortable; damp, lumpy. But there I was, magicked inside a tree trunk and there was nothing I could do about it.

It was a long time before she gave up trying to reach me, poking about in knot-holes and snapping twigs, but at last she shambled off, cursing all the way.

'Let me out!' I cried again.

'Oh, Yaffingale,' murmured the elder, 'only the truth will set you free.'

*

Looking back on it, I hardly understood the difficulty of my situation. There I was, trapped in a tree-trunk, safe from the enchantress, admittedly – but at the mercy of that other magical being, the elder. And I had no idea whether it had my best interests at heart.

'Let me out!' I said. 'You can't keep me in here.' This was nonsense, of course. It absolutely could keep me in there. It could keep me until I starved. The enchantress might have survived without food and drink, but as an ordinary, mortal woodpecker, I could not.

'The witch thinks you have put an enchantment upon her and she blames me! That's not right.'

'We must tell the truth,' said the elder. It had acquired a nasty tone lately.

I had told it no lies, but I hadn't told it everything. Those sins of omission were about to find me out.

'I will if you will,' I said. That was brave. No, it was foolhardy. 'You haven't told me everything, have you?'

The tree was silent awhile. There was nothing I could do but wait, pushing my wings against the damp wood, trying to make a little more space. But I was held fast.

'Very well,' said the elder at last. 'I have used you, and the enchantress, too, to achieve my ends.'

No wonder she's so cross, I thought.

'You will remember, Yaffingale, when we first met, I told you how she came to be trapped in my trunk. There was a plague in the rye-fields, and the people blamed her for it. I rescued her from being burned as a witch. Very decent of me, was it not?

As I recalled, the elder was rescuing itself from the flames, too, but this wasn't the moment to remind it.

'Well,' the elder went on, 'she was so volatile I couldn't let her out, so I got to know her pretty well. And, dash it all, she admitted she was indeed responsible for the plague in the rye-fields. Nothing accidental about it. Sheer spitefulness on her part. She's a nasty piece of work, you know.'

'Tell me about it,' I muttered.

'All that time she was in my trunk, I absorbed much of her knowledge and some of her magical powers, too.'

'Why didn't she try to break the spell herself?'

'Oh, she tried. But it did her no good. Anyway,' said the elder, 'it gave me an idea. You have spoken with the trees. You told me yourself they were self-centred and miserable. Isolation, you see. It's a real disadvantage being stuck in the ground by the roots. You don't get about much. I reckoned they'd all be happier if they could communicate more, share resources, that sort of thing.'

'The ash-tree said its ancestor had uprooted itself and climbed a mountain,' I pointed out.

'Nonsense,' said the elder. 'Just trying to make itself look superior. Now where was I? Oh, yes. I thought to release the witch and get her to do the job for me.'

'How could you persuade her to do that?' She hadn't struck me as the public-spirited type.

'Aha,' said the elder, very sly. 'I, um, made a few modifications to her magical powers while she was trapped in my trunk. In short, she doesn't know she's been helping me.'

That made sense.

'So what has she done for you, your honour? Does it have anything to do with the toadstools?'

'Not as stupid as you look, are you, Yaffingale? Yes, I used the fact that she could spread that fungal plague in the rye, adapted it so she trailed helpful fungi from tree to tree

She had sworn revenge on all trees after being held captive by me. Ver y vocal about it.

71

I used that to my advantage, to the forest's advantage. I knew she'd go round them all. Worked a treat, if I may say so. I'm getting excellent reports from all round the forest. Trees are talking to each other through the fungi, supporting each other, just as I planned.'

'But the toadstools only appear in autumn, mostly,' I said. 'What about the rest of the year?'

'That's the beauty of it,' said the elder. 'The fungus network is underground. You can't see it, but it's always there, working away. The toadstools are just the fruits.'

'What about the fungi bursting out of the trunks? Some of them are pretty nasty.'

'All down to the enchantress,' said the elder. 'Nothing to do with me. But I think a few parasites are a small price to pay for this wonderful communication system, don't you?'

I'd have shrugged if I'd had the room.

'Now will you let me out?' I said.

'I admit I didn't tell you about the talking toadstools. Some of them sang at me, you know. Thought you'd think I was crazy, that's all.

But you knew all about them anyway, so it hardly matters, does it? So let me out!'

'No,' said the elder.

'What do you mean, no?'

'I mean I can't. The spell for magicking you and the witch into my trunk requires a willing individual to work the release mechanism. You let her out, willingly. Only she can let you out. It's a sort of fail-safe, you see.'

*

This was a whole new level of complication.

I knew the only reason she'd let me out willingly would be so she could get a clear shot at me.

'How can I get her to do it peaceably?' I asked.

'Let's see,' said the elder. 'Why did you let her out?'

'I didn't really want to. She's intimidating,' I said.

'Agreed,' said the elder. 'Perhaps you should try intimidating her.'

'Me? How can I do that?'

'I've already given you the means to do that,' said the elder. I hate it when trees go all mysterious on you. What had the elder told me? Sometimes, even now I'm much older and wiser, I am still surprised by the depth of my stupidity. But not as often as I was then.

'Oh. You said she had admitted to spreading the rye-plague.'

'Excellent,' said the elder. 'You're learning, Yaffingale. She's guilty as charged. The village people got very nasty with her when they merely suspected she was responsible. Supposing they knew for sure? Her powers are much weaker among human beings, you know – she's three-parts human herself.'

I imagined the fourth part was something very grumpy indeed.

'But I can't talk to humans,' I said. 'She must know that. How can I threaten to expose her guilt?'

The elder-tree shivered all its remaining leaves in an impatient sigh, so they flew and fluttered away.

'I am a magical tree. I can enable you to talk to human beings. It's a simple spell. Hocus, pocus. There, it's done.'

I felt something strange happening to my beak and throat. The elder was truly more powerful than I had thought.

'I can really talk to humans now?' I croaked. It did sound odd.

'Of course,' said the elder. 'Now, I'll call the enchantress, shall I, and we'll get you out. The toadstools will transmit the message for me. Much as I enjoy your company, I'd just as soon you were on the outside.'

'You and me both,' I said, very hoarse.

I was still coming to terms with being a woodpecker that could talk to humans when the enchantress returned.

'Master Yaffingale is under my protection,' said the elder, 'but we would both be grateful if you'd just let him out.'

'Why should I?' The enchantress had her arms tightly folded. 'He's been a confounded nuisance.'

'Tell her, Yaffingale.'

'Um, the elder has given me magical powers,' I said, as pompous as possible. 'I can talk to humans. I can tell them you spread the rye-plague.'

She went quiet and the whole forest seemed to hold its breath. Even the toadstools stopped chattering.

'I might have had something to do with it,' she said at last.

'You had everything to do with it,' I said. 'Now let me out.'

'Free him,' added the elder, who was thinking more clearly than I was, 'and I'll reverse the spell. Shut him up. You have my solemn vow to that, and you know I can't break it. Otherwise, I leave the spell and he'll tell the first person that passes by. The village will hunt you down without mercy.'

The enchantress hesitated a moment, then rushed forward and pressed the new mark on the back of the elder's trunk. I shot out and flew as fast as I could. She threw a half-hearted thunderbolt after me.

*

A day or so later, I returned warily to the elder, keeping my distance.

The Mark
on the Bark

deception

'Safe and sound?' it asked, very matter of fact.

'Yes,' I said, 'but I would like to have tried talking to humans. Did you really break the spell?'

'I never put it on,' said the elder.

'Pardon?'

'I don't have that power. Made it all up. But you believed it. You sounded very convincing, if I may say so. And the enchantress couldn't take the risk. That little symbol on my trunk...'

'It means deception,' I said, without thinking. 'I can read them, you know.'

'Something else you never told me you could do,' said the elder, 'Just as well you took no notice of it. I deceived both of you.'

'Has she really gone?'

'Yes, moved on to another forest.'

'Good riddance.'

'What she may not realise,' said the elder confidentially, 'is that she will continue to spread the toadstool network. Wherever there are trees they will be united; talking, sharing, supporting one another through the web of fungi.

76

Rather ingenious, though I say so myself. You will note all the trees, even me, now have a new symbol on our trunks: can you tell me what it signifies, clever clogs?'

'Yes,' I said. All the old marks were gone, replaced by a single new one. 'It means blessings.'

'Just so,' said the elder-tree, and I could have sworn it chuckled.

'Hoo, hoo, very clever,' said a voice as I flew away.

On the ground, on the dead stumps, the toadstools were chuckling. The trees had stopped being miserable and were chuckling too. The whole forest was chuckling. I chuckled, too. But then, I'm a green woodpecker and laughing is what I do best.

'Ha, ha, ha,' I called as I flew away.

*

In time I realised I had learned much from the trees' tales and become a wiser woodpecker. My last encounter with the enchantress and the elder had shown me many things – the value of protection when I was within the trunk of the tree; a thing or two about the nature of justice when the enchantress paid for her wrong-doing by right-doing; the doubtful benefits of interventions by man; the futility of trying to escape destiny, and the wonders of my journey from ignorance to wisdom.

Oh, and I also learned that blessings can come in very unexpected forms, including that of a clump of toadstools.

The End